THE ETERNAL SHIP

A Novella By Chris Godber

ABOUT THE AUTHOR

Chris has written poems since his youth, writes regularly for coding magazine iC0de as well as producing short stories and writing philosophical essays for London Based artists collective The Tunnel.

He also has experience teaching English as a foreign language for two years to Russian Students at a camp called Rekaleto near Moscow, Russia.

Most recently Chris released two compilations of short stories called 'Suicide by Computation' and Romance in the Commieblocks. The Eternal Ship is his first novella.

He is the Director of Alien Rabbit Limited, a British Indie publisher of original fiction and graphic novels alongside co-director Naima Valli.

Chris enjoys programming, painting, drawing and coffee.

THE ETERNAL SHIP

A Novella by Chris Godber

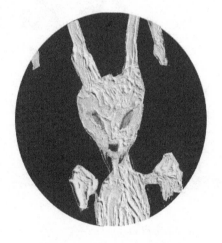

ISBN: 978-1-7391474-5-7

PUBLISHED BY
ALIEN RABBIT LIMITED

The fool who persists in his folly will become wise.

-William Blake

1. Edition, 2022

© 2022 All rights reserved.

ALIEN RABBIT LIMITED

THE ETERNAL SHIP

Table of Contents

BOUNDLESS LOVE

They gathered cold like hard stones on a harsh winter evening around the campfire as the flames flickered and rose in the darkness of the night. Sheltered together they sat around its sacred flame, to feel the warmth of being; gathered around the heat like so many before them had to stave off the cold harsh numbness of the darkness surrounding them in the snow. Travellers of the tunnels, the windows to the soul within - Artists of the divine spirit whose light beacon glowed brightly from the Eternal Ship.

They stared from a window, looking glass self out into the world again, huddled in their ideals, to look out at the herd below and let out a collective chuckle that would chill the bones of most mortal men, a laughter heavy with a sense of existential dread and the inner knowledge of what it was to suffer. Souls half dead languishing in the living pigment, their eyes glowing white with delight, frozen in time eternal staring through the canvas threads at their audience below, frozen in time - ghosts.

All who had seen the harsh light of The Eternal were forever branded, cursed to wander together, bandits of the advance guard, comrades of the new persuasion, warriors of the new entombed forever in the dull realities of the present.

A male figure shrouded in darkness and covered in a thick woolly tunic sat in the corner furthest from the campfire and put his hand upon his beard and began to stroke it thought- fully, almost too intentionally;

'Ahhh what sweet mystery it is to stare upon them, so at peace with eternity, never seeing its true face as we have;

Those burning eyes of hot crimson coals which burrow under the skin, how pleasant it must be - ahhh to never feel this frozen solemnity. To be free from this pain we endured and overcame'

'Oh please spare me your pontificating would you Maximo! Does everything have to be so full of man's hubris, so head and no heart? Relax please...' the long-suffering woman to his right said with a shake of her head.

'Why, of course — for it is in the texture and pattern of one's bones where the truth of wherever a man is a man can be told'

'Please, the all too familiar lecture, you know I have heard it too many times to mention.' complained the woman, rolling her eyes as she looked at him in the eyes with relegated loving indifference, her languid blue hair flickering in the wind. It was no time for arguments, and if eternity taught you anything, it was that it was rarely worth the effort to argue the same old points to death.

Further away though, through the labyrinths of infinite space and time, in a chamber made of marble, in a cathedral of art and culture, a middle-aged man with a pot-belly and a thick brown moustache, small glasses and tiny beady eyes was talking to his class of students. The eternal couple peered out of their canvas thread and looked down as he began to speak methodically and in perfect deadpan metronome.

'And now class, look upon the figure here, She is Julia Zinovev - the tortured poet of the steppes, painter of the contemplative, cursed with a deep depression. A depression and curse that haunted her and her entire group of comrades 'The Eternal Ship' for the entirety of their radical, fiery and turbulent existence.

See how the skilled eye of an artist captured her mercurial, sensual form with a strong graphic line, her sensuality all radiating in the eyes, rendered with light brush marks.' The smartly dressed man paused for a second adjusting his tight tie awkwardly. 'Winking at you though the magic of the canvas itself you could say! And not to forget the way the artist Maximo Zinoev, her Husband in art and life, rendered the beautiful blue of her hair, see there how the artist made it shimmer with a excellent use of the dry brush technique that makes it look like the surface of a brilliant blue ocean itself'

The children looked back at their Art teacher Alexey with inattention, distracted by the stimulating wonder of all the paintings before them, showing them the windows of the world soul. Light pouring in from the eternal. Sculptures for the boys to follow to the eternal muses, who they perused with excited enthusiasm and for the young girls who gathered in small groups to dream of a beautiful tomorrow - shining in the light of true equality – self-expression and freedom, life beyond the fields of toil, and the ever present washing basin.

'Sir, all that is well and good, but what is the Eternal ship?' a young boy asked out loudly as he raised his hand quickly from the middle of the group of young teenagers.

'Ahhh yes Konstantin, well let me tell you a story boys and girls, of how a gang of desperate and brilliant artists and dreamers had the tenacity to dream that they may one day make the world a better place, and through struggle and strife, that dream came true, and all right here – in this great city, our great city of Moscow but 30 years ago, when she lay in ruins'

The class focused on Alexey suddenly, drawn to the fire that pulsated in his language, taking them to a story that would both inspire, horrify and give form to our highest shared humanity, to the depths of our darkest fears and the worst of our natures.

"It began in the year 2080 and in the semi-derelict streets of an outer suburb in Moscow called the Meshchansky District, which was a simple and barren urban landscape...

A tall and dishevelled man with golden curly hair like a messy lion wearing an unironed black shirt and a crooked maroon red tie, stood on a street corner. A group of 20 people had gathered around him in the winter cold as he broadcast his voice over their morning chattering.

'And if I shall be wounded, defending what is right – our right to strike! Well why should I care, they have taken everything from us, they don't give us our fair pay, they don't grant us our human rights and they expect it all, our sweat and the toil of our labour! What have we been given in return for our work, for our hours given, the time has come friends, to fight them back! Fight back against the government, give us back our right to strike! "

'Fight back? With what? Our damp shoes?' A voice snorted from the back as the small crowd began sniggering and sneering loudly at Maximo, whose strong frame began to cower and falter on the makeshift stage.

The Man froze like a statue in time, before blurting out the regretful words

'ummm, with ummm with hmmm ughhhh, with Art!' he suddenly vomited out of his throat like a reflex, as if he were a toad hiccuping in a cold pond, desperate for company, croaking pathetically.

The roar of laughter from the crowd was palpable and spread like wildfire, as Maximo became downcast, turning beetroot red and making for the exit in shame, his face red as he looked to the ground and plotted his hasty escape. Pushing past the bemused faces that surrounded him, and the mocking voices, he felt he wanted the ground to swallow him up whole, so that he could dissolve into the background again - sweet anonymity.

'Enough of this politics, it is time for art - time to return to the studio.' And so Maximo walked with intent towards his small apartment studio a few blocks up the road, before a voice called out from behind him, breaking his daydreaming.

'Hello, Hello, please before you depart' the voice of a young woman pierced through the whirlwind of terrifying public embarrassment, as Maximo looked up from his shameful hiding, stopping suddenly as he pulled away from the hostile mumbling crowd surrounding him.

'I heard what you said, and I must say I broadly agree; culture and revolution cannot be separate from one another and they both must cradle the light of the other, that was the gist of what you were saying - right?' The woman said standing and smiling sweetly, reciting her insights to Maximo who stood for a sublime second and felt utter opioid-like bliss, yet with none of the terrible downfall or hunger.

'Was there finally someone who could see it too? Another who had seen the light of that eternal ship that came to him in dreams night upon night?' Maximo wondered as he began to open his mouth to speak to the woman who stood before him, resplendent already in his mind as an intellectual equal, as well as a woman of great physical beauty.

'I'm glad at least someone understood what I was saying out there, is it really so hard to see how we can.... umm I'm sorry, forgive me I'm afraid I have forgotten to ask your name, what is it?"

'I am Julia, Artist, Poet and woman of the Steppes'

'Ahhh Julia, as Jupiter your namesake, powerful she may be' thought Maximo before extending his hand to greet her and giving it a quick kiss.

"And I am Maximo! Philosopher, Notorious Fool of the district, writer and painter of dreams"

'And what do your parents call you then Max?' Julia sighed looking at Max with heavy tired eyes full of flame.

'They call me hopeless'

'Feckless for me' she responded

'Artist' they both said at the same time as they began cackling wildly.

'Let's go for a drink'

RENDEZVOUS

"The beer here is a kind of swivel but it is cheap at least" Max lamented staring at Julia who took a quick sip of the unbranded lager before her.

'Well when you are as poor as us you can't afford to be too picky, and besides too much of this stuff isn't so good for you, so well dammit it's good to suffer so that you don't well suffer, a very Russian logic wouldn't you agree Max?'

Max's usual frowning expression broke and a sly smile widened on his face as he began to laugh

'Well that is certainly true haha' he laughed out loud, the tension broken in the air as she burned through his outer cynic to the fool that lived beneath, laughing in ecstatic joy at the very absurdity of existence. 'And what brought you here Julia? A woman of the steppes? I would very much like to see your work as well, please tell me more'

'Well it's quite a simple story, the old clichés of course.'

Julia had a tone of bemusement in her voice as Max looked at her with a distant look as if analysing the contours of her face 'perhaps he has already chosen me as a muse' she chuckled to herself internally with pitch perfect poker face. 'And what are these clichés my dear, I am sure I know nothing of such things' Max said with a knowing glint in his eye.

'Well I was bought up in the steppes, a woman of the countryside, abusive Father who wanted a boy, only child, disgraceful rebel, political radical, tortured artist, all true of course in one way or the other, but really I wanted to broaden my horizons, to see more of the world, there is so much world to paint, so much to see and experience - a certain wanderlust compels me into all the places where the rebuilding is at its most vital...'

Max listened with intent as she relayed her story, pausing in his trance to nod now and again as he stared deeply into her deep brown eyes and started to become lost, melting into her soul. They chatted of the war, they talked of the ruinous times, the danger and death they had witnessed and overcame to get them to this point - their apex point of creativity.

'It was such a terrible time wasn't it Julia, vast swathes of the city aflame, vast fields in chaos, such destruction, such meaningless destruction and death. I myself served for a time as a war journalist. I had the unfortunate task of simply and merely recording it all. Condemned to the showreel, crucified to the digital display. A kind of death of sorts...'

'Oh Max it was surely a difficult time, but we can be glad it has passed now' Julia said clutching Maximo's hand.

'And we after all must now look to the future, look to art like you said, build the new world from the ashes, we've been here before, and we may well be here again. I know for myself what it is feel crushed from the inside, the pressure can become too much sometimes' She extended out her hand to Max whose eyes were distant and locked into some eternal terrible moment, as his hand shook a little from distant unspoken memories. She took his hand and held it firmly.

'Whatever you saw, whatever you were forced to endure, I know I have a good sense for people, a deep instinct for the good, and you are a good man.' Max looked deeply into her eyes with his battle hardened tired old face, his lion's mane of hair exposed , greying and vulnerable and gripped her firm hand with his own. It felt like a holy frozen moment, the type that seldom arises, but which accentuate the divine moments of existence. 'Thank you, Julia, thank you, and I think you are right, we must not relinquish hope, we must keep faith in the reformation, keep on the course of creation. Render nothing but the simple truth'

'I agree, I like you Max, this all feels very sudden but would you like to stay the night at my residence' She inquired with widening eyes

"What cloud have you descended down from, sweet angel?" Max smiled softly.

'I would love to, if you would have me!'

And they walked out hand in hand from the Dive bar.

CONQUEST?

Julia lived in an apartment down a back alley of Moscow, the roads there were always badly maintained and the private company that was supposed to be repairing them were always short of eligible men. Julia and Maximo raced off down the streets with light feet, making sure to avoid the bumps and holes that marked their path. As they ran past, adepts of the tech god Mansu surrounded them and gave their daily sacrifices of circuitry and cable, inserting the cards into the idol's bizarre mechanised mouth. 'So Maximo, your place or mine?' Julia whispered under the shadow of a Mansu idol, its metallic skin glistening in the magic of the moon's light as she smiled with a mischievous grin on her face, and Maximo began to blush.

'Let's go to your place' Maximo said blushing deeply, his face redder than a late dawn sun, burning its light out.

'I live up on the corner of Vasneya Street, up there you see in that small bottom floor apartment, that one Maximo - with the flag outside you see?'

'Ahhh the flag, yes, what does it mean? With the black and the circular icon It looks a bit like the pirate flag I have seen before in stories but somehow more hopeful, more good-natured.

'It is the flag of our secret club - The Eternal Ship'

'Our secret club Julia?'

'Yes, me and my son, see I live here with my son'

'You mean you were married once before? Or had a lover?'

'Don't look so surprised Maximo, you are not the only man in the world or in my life, but right now you are the only one I am looking at' Maximo sighed and let his world-weary smile sing its solemn song.

'And I could do with a good rogering from a Black Beard' chuckled Julia

'Oh ah!' shouted Maximo as they ran up the stairs to Julia's bed.

Daylight broke on The Eternal Ship as Max opened his eyes on a fresh morning, and felt for the first time in a long time a sense of peace and happiness entering his bones again, so tired from all the activism, the yearning for the better world. Had he perhaps forgotten to look after himself in the process? Julia would help of course, and she had already, nourishing his world-weary frame with some confidence and care.

'Ahh so you're up already'

Her face popped up from the pillows as she rubbed her nose onto his which filled Maximo with a sense of long forgotten joy. 'Yeah, what time is it? Perhaps I need to paint I think today, I feel so re-energised'

'Thanks to?'

'Why you of course!'

'That's right boy, now don't you forget it'

They sniggered together.

'Ahh Julia you said you were a poet? I would love to read your poetry if you'll permit me to some time.

'Poetry is a private act for me Maximo, you must give me time, and then I will reveal my whole face, but for now I would like you to meet someone who is very special to me, if you are willing?'

Maximo felt a little apprehensive 'Of course I will meet him, how do I look?'

'Get your pants on, shower and comb your hair, then you can meet my little one'

THE CLOWN OF MANSU

'How many times must I tell them, how many lives must I take, till they see my card fully revealed'

'Ahaha, Clown!" The word stung like a whip from Mansu again.

"You fool! What are you doing? Daydreaming again you clown, pay attention for the sake of Mansu, fool!"

Mother was moaning in the room above again, nagging in the way that all mothers do.

'Ok, well I apologise'

'Your apologies aren't enough you fool, get out of my sight" she shouted down to the clown, languishing in his basement room.

'One day I will show you mother that you should not play with the sight of a clown, time to write into my journal again, time to laugh and retire to my lab.'

The Clown had a name so ordinary that it burned into the Clowns soul. 'Mother, damn you, you lamentable bitch'

'Out of my sight fool, get out of here you foolish boy, get out of my sight'

'Fucking bitch.'

The Clown ran to his hiding spot and sought solace amongst the circuits, more sacrifices for Mansu. The machine God looked down on him from above and cackled with its slimy mechanical fangs baring down on the slave before him, with sadistic glee. "But Slave, I need more, we need to build our ship into the black kingdom, the singularity that takes all things...."

'But master, have I not provided enough, all these treasures, all these organs, all the hearts I bring you to engorge your endless lust, have I not done enough for you, suffered enough?"

'There is no end to suffering Adept'

The slave was alone, alone with just the harsh voices of the Gods in his head for company as he began to write into his journal;

I know that I am utterly insane, that I am a mad monk, a perverted killer and a rat to all of humanity, I cannot escape my fate, that fate is to serve, to sacrifice to the great Mansu, the beast that is me and without, my guilt; I must run from my ruin"

'Then sacrifice once more' the voice commanded

'No, please Mansu no, no" he lamented with tears welling in his eyes 'Please I beg you Mansu spare me from my terrible fate.'

`You must do it for me, we must build our ship to the warp fields beyond this world, all great sacrifices require many circuits, many wires, and this doll you bring before us is of no significance in the grand plan."

The doll was in the corner, with two wires forcibly inserted into her eyes. The Clown had brutally screwed them in earlier, as he began his new collection.

"Thank Mansu that the old bitch has not noticed the stench yet, at least she lets me keep this basement for my experiments' the clown sniggered to himself.

"Son!, come back up here now, that Priest is visiting you for the first time this afternoon, make yourself presentable"

"Yes, Mother"

'I shall be making you a doll soon' the clown thought as the woman in the corner grimaced in her death mask, trapped in an eternal moon grimace.

Suddenly the doorbell rang;

'Ahh greetings, I'm from the temple, and I'm here to check in on your son and assess his suitability for missionary work, can I come in?'

'Of course you may enter Adept, the boy is in his basement, playing with his toys as usual'

'Such is the way with many lost men his age" grinned the priest with kindness, not knowing the horror that lay within this house of mirrors, the decaying dolls that lay beneath.

'Boy,your Priest is here, come up and say hello' Mothers voice rang out from above.

'Coming mother'

'Oh it's ok, I can visit him in his room'

'No. You cannot' she responded bluntly 'No one may enter that pit except for him.'

'That is a little overprotective if you don't mind me saying, he can't stay lost in his fantasies forever, that is why the missionary work will be good for him, we have a little bit of a mixed reputation as an emerging cult at the minute, but we are focused on reforming men who have turned away from the light of the great machine owl's eyes, returning them back to wisdom and the great work of Mantor'

'I have heard it before, it sounds like the Christianity my late Father practised, so tell me Priest, is there a heaven in this great owl's kingdom?'

'Well, It's not quite as simple as that'

'So Hell then?'

She whispered as her son entered the room with a sense of palatable rage resonating from him;

'Why all these interruptions, I was playing with my Dolls mother! My dolls! I am working on a great project, and when I am done I shall be worshipped as I deserve'

His face was strange and contorted as if he wore a black veil over his face, his eyes aflame with delusion, and the Priest felt it clear as day.

'Hello son, I am Alexey from the Temple and I have been assigned to you to act as your mentor, I will be guiding you in the ways of Temple life, and in how to live a good and prosperous life, we are a people that believe in service to others via our lord Mansu - some tales tell of the ancient origins of this word. I can tell you the origin of Mantor and his Father Mansu if you wish?'

'I can hear it, but I know it already' the clown chuckled looking at his mother with a bemused expression, projecting an unearned arrogance as she looked back at him with a look of thinly veiled disgust. 'Long before form there was the void, nothing existed in the world except for the infinite circle of chaos, this circle was formless and would spin around and around in revolutions in the void that would render the inhabitants below mere pawns in the hands of the Gods; looking down from above, who would laugh and plan the next turning of the circle for their own amusement.

That was all before Mansu, Mansu came before all the Gods and said no more, I just need as many wires as possible and I can build us the highest temple of all temples, I just need our people to dig deep into the earth, to find the wires that will light it and we may become as the very Gods themselves.'

'Our lord Mansu came down in humanoid form during the great war to initiate the great work, incarnating in the form of the one you must know by now.'

'You mean him'

The clown pointed to a portrait of Mantor hovering above the kitchen table.

'Yes, Mantor, our lord and our protector, the divine warrior within, struck down during the final battle in the defence of

Moscow - he extolled the virtue of building, of mutual respect and ingenuity - of the power of our wires to extend into the sky above so that we may build a new world. Bless him and his sacrifice, Long live Mantor!'

'Yes, Long live our lord Alexey, and I have already gathered some sacrifices for our lord amongst the rust aha!'

'Can I see what circuits you have gathered then, dear boy, so that I may exchange them for coins at the temple?'

'Next time 'Priest, time to leave'

Mother was clearly not pleased to have this man snooping around, and so the Adept left and returned to his notebooks and night study.

Alexey sat down to a tough night's work;

'So this man, his name is so similar to mine, yet so different in character I feel somehow. He seems like a strange man, so consumed in a dreamlike bubble as to be blind to the rest of the world, and why the overprotective aspect of the mother? That made little sense. Alexey lit his cigarette and sat back in his chair.

'But still I shouldn't give up on him, even one as seemingly degenerated as him, that is surely what Mantor would have done in such a situation' he thought as he glimpsed at a portrait of Mantor hanging on his wall, staring at him with worn, tired yet determined eyes.

And so he opened the man's file on his monitor and began his investigations;

Name: [REDACTED] Age: 42

Occupation: Unemployed due to [REDACTED]

Description: [REDACTED] is afflicted with an unknown mental health condition and lives with his Mother at their residence. He is currently unemployed but has said he would like to work as a doctor, or join the local division of the Temple of Mansu as a missionary on the path to being an Adept, where he has stated, and I quote that he would like to 'help young girls turn into mature living dolls'. I am personally cautious to recommend this course of action to the welfare department, given his past criminal record, which I am unable to mention in this letter, but I have left it to the local council to determine his fate and I hope they make the right decision.

Signed

Dr Petrovich

Alexey didn't need to read it twice, he felt an intuition about what the redacting could mean, he always found such men a horror to work with, impossible and endlessly deluded, probably beyond saving - definitely deranged.

'What could be in this for him or even for this man who was clearly already lost. He could make a suitable factory or manual worker perhaps, but he could never be let near anyone vulnerable. The welfare department were clearly fobbing him off to the foot soldiers of Mantor.' That's the reformation for you thought Alexey bitterly. Alexey picked up his microphone and dialled into the local Moscow council line.

'Moscow Employment line, how can I help?' 'Hi, it's Alexey calling regarding the man whom I was sent to assess today by the employment office, I am sorry, but we really cannot have anyone with his tendencies and condition within our sacred order, please pass on Mantor's thanks and blessings but he is is simply probably too disturbed to find a place in our temple and I believe it is in everyone's best interest that he be kept away from the vulnerable. Mansu forgive him in the next life, because he is beyond forgiveness in this one'

The line operator listened intently, her face contorting in silent horror as she listened to the Adepts word down the line.

'I'll make sure to pass that on to the director, thank you very much Mr Alexey, Mantor be with you too'

And Mantor started smiling from the wall, knowing that Alexey had made the right choice as he lit another cigarette and sighed in the warm glimmer of his Adepts hovel.

THE SECRET, POLICE.

'Julia I have something to tell you..'

'What's that my love?'

'When I told you I was an artist, it was a half-truth at best, and a complete lie at worst'

'Why is that, oh go on tell me, I am sure I can take it'

'I'm an artist, but that's moonlighting for me, I am a Private Detective by day and an artist by night'

'Well it pays well I assume dear?'

"That it can"

'Well then what's the problem? I am short of cash and you can provide, you can provide, can't you Max?'

'Yes I have a few cases I can take on at the minute on the job board and I just finished a few minor jobs, maybe I should show them to you, get your opinion, which I would value a lot, truly.'

Case number 1: Adept of the Mansu reported about a dubious man exhibiting psychotic features which gave cause for concern - can pay per hour Case Number 2: Missing children - children are starting to go missing around the woods on the Southside of Moscow for the past 3 days - The Parents of Concern - we will make sure to pay you upon the safe return of our children. Case Number 3: It's me ahaha :

I am he hahaha I am Mantors' nemesis ahaha

I will pay you with our lovely lions den ahahaha I am so alone and only he provides the answer ahaha MUM MUM Case Number 4: Join the Police

The Moscow Police Force are looking for private contractors for an ongoing investigation in the area - good wage. Solid ½ year contract.

'Well this is too obvious' chuckled Max 'These are all the same case, these are all connected.'

'Missing Children Max' 'Hmm' Max sighed looking at Julia with inquisitive eyes

'There are children going missing Max' Julia's eyes suddenly filled with fear

'You know what to do.'

Maximo curtly nodded and with a heavy heart donned his heavy winter jacket and headed outside into the cold unforgiving night and visited the local police station, to sign himself up to the only case in town - Who is Mantor's Nemesis?

'I will be gone a while my love, but I will send you coin when I can'

'Love you' Julia said softly with a grin

'I love you too' sighed Max as he exited their new home with a feeling of sadness entering his bones. 'And tell the boy I love him as well' Max smiled as he closed the door.

Julia felt the sadness immediately, her heart full of a great sorrow that burned into her breast as her hero left, and she returned to her drawer full of his paintings and essays, poems and photographs collected over several years. "Please, please protect my sweet angel, oh Mantor for it is for you that I am, and you that we all are. Mere slaves no more, protect my sweet one out there in the wilds of the wind, I give him my heart, my soul, my everything so that he may stop the monster haunting us..... For the great light, for the world soul, for all mankind, this great evil must stop.'

Julia suddenly thought she heard a whisper in the wind 'He is the Great Owl' She began to write into her journal of poems, her book of silent pain which she kept deep in the roots of the Earth of her soul. He is the Great Owl,

His hoots. it's ravenous amongst the clouds   Protects and provides;' He is the great Owl

He keeps guard

My tears shall not swell his growing - In my heart.

Tears streamed down Julia's eyes until they subsided, her soul now cleansed by poetry and the powerful pen, Her spirit of the woods danced with her, and she was again the fae spirit within - resplendent and exquisite.

'Maximo Ivanavich?' 'Yes that is my name'

'Sign here, here and here. Welcome to the Police force son'

'I have been here before you know'

'Well I don't want to know what for hey then sir haha well better get you to the black hats then right?' 'Well I suppose it's so' smiled Max 'And not for the first time, God what was I thinking saying that out loud' Max was lead up the metallic stairs, a little bit rusty from years of corrosion and neglect into a semi derelict office adorned with framed pictures of officers and a man sat in a leather chair, reclining and looking out the window puffing on a cigar with a glass of whisky to his side.

'So you are the new guy huh?'

The Captain said looking at Max with inquisitive eyes

'Come and join me for a whiskey then son, and let's chat about what's going on, and you'll need the whiskey believe me...'

'So what's your name'

'Sorry to be informal sir, but I don't know yours yet'

'Ahh me? Peter, Peter Volkov" Max suddenly stiffened like a board with respect to the man that sat before him.

"Peter Volkov! Well I am honoured sir, and they call me Maximo but you can call me Max" Max extended his hand and with a firm handshake shook the hand of Peter the Great. 'So how did you crack the infamous case?'

'I had to understand on some level, I had to get into the heads of those gangsters, to face evil itself right in the eye, to tell it no there is a limit. It took blood, it took sweat and it took tears, but we got the bastards in the end'

;That you did sir, and may they forever rot in hell;

;Then we are of like mind son, and we shall now speak as equals, now please do take a seat Max whilst I tell you of the unfortunate case we have before us, a case I can't take to my usual guys, family issues you know the drill;

'I do Boss, that I do' Max sighed as he took a sip of the fine scotch before him.

'You mind?' Max said rolling a cigarette with the tobacco from his jacket.

'The fuck you asking me for?'

Sniggered Peter 'I'm Peter the Great for fuck's sake light your cigarette man' and they both erupted into laughter.

'Now Max we gotta get onto the serious business, and my friend I have to warn you this is a heavy one, as heavy as it gets, heavier than any sin you or I may have on our souls'

'I know unfortunately what this is regarding, I read in the advert of course'

'Alright so tell me, why are these missing children worth investigating?'

'Because they are missing'

Peter looked sad for a moment and stared deeply into Max's eyes 'You got any children Max?'

'That's a long story boss, I might have one now, but like I said it's a long story'

'I know what you mean boy, you got yourself a keeper it sounds like, now anyway we know this language, we know how this works, there is no point thinking the worst yet, we were children once we know what life was like then, you get in a gang, you make a den, you go on crazy quests, you sneak out into the woods when you think no-one is looking..'

'And there can be bears in the woods.'

'Shit, damn it man I said don't think the worst, but of course I have considered that, so we'll work on the assumption that there could be a case here, do a search of the woods south of the city barriers, I've assembled a team of my finest, most experienced officers to escort you and we start immediately, here is your badge, and I'm assigning you a partner, who you will meet later today'

'Of course sir, thank you' Max nodded as the sense of enormity began weighing on his shoulders. 'If this turns out to be something sinister, we are going to need men like you'

'Men like me sir?'

Max said his thoughts lost in investigation already

'Men who can peer into the blackest holes in men, understand it and help deliver justice'

The two men nodded to each other and Max left the room with a sense of alertness and palpitations already rising in his heart. 'And Max? Drill it down with the sour face, huh? A little pessimism is natural, but try to remember why you got into this damn filthy business in the first place huh, that helps me I find, along with the Whisky.'

'Oh I remember well enough, I remember why and how I got into this filthy business. It was all blown upon by me, and I felt the lash for it alright' Max was in his new agency car driving at a medium speed towards the woods through the suburbs as the sun began to lower, its orange glow replaced by the endless night, snow piling up on the side roads, ill winds and sad hearts. 'Max! Max! Watch out! Watch out!'

'Huh' Max had suddenly started drifting off at the wheel a second 'Hey man keep your eye on the road, shit am I partnered up with a goddamn junkie again or something'

'Hey watch your mouth man, I was just getting lost in some memories a minute'

'Well watch your memories don't reduce us to snowmush, you haven't spoken a goddamn word since we left base, what is that at least?'

'Maximo'

'Fuck, The Maximo? Moscow Max?!'

'Yes, Moscow Max, who blew the war report wide open.' Max spluttered out the well rehearsed answer.

'Shit man now I can see why you don't open up easily'

'Life can make you distrust people, but I have an escape'

'Oh yeah what is that then?'

'Art, I paint pictures'

'Ah ok, well that's fair enough, each of us needs a hobby that's for sure.'

Max felt a hidden tear welling in his eye - 'a hobby, I am not tired of hearing that one' as he sped off into the woods focused on his goal, and thinking of Julia as he puffed on his cigarette at the wheel.

'My new doll she is being painted up as I think, what colour shall I paint her today, Malush?"

the fingers wrote down on the parchment before him as he sat in his basement twitching with excitement. 'Oh red Malush, oh it shall be done oh Malush Malush doll above'

'Are you playing with your dolls again!?' His mother growled from above 'Leave me be mother, I am doing my great work'

'You are a freak son, and it would have haunted your Father to see what you have become' 'Be gone!'

he shouted as he initiated the triple lock on his door.

'We'll be here a while'

She looked at the monster with terrified eyes and wept as the colour red was applied to her skin with his toxic hands. ;I shall paint for Malush all the colours of the rainbow my little one' he smiled cruelly.

Maximo felt a pull in his mind to a place unknown to him as he drove down the cold dark road, the place he had hid before, to the tent in the woods, the covers he lay under to hide from the noise outside.

`You really do live in your head man'

Maximo was starting to find his partner's presence most tiresome. 'I do, and you, what's your name partner?' Max smirked 'Transfer in from the US, Jackson at your service, I'm a half mad contractor. Just like you, it seems'

'Ahh now I see why your English is so good, well hello Jackson, and welcome to our little province of chaos, do you have a first name?'

'Just Jack, I'm Jack Jackson'

'Your parents must have had a sick sense of humour'

'What makes you say that?'

Maximo looked at Jack Jackson with a grin 'I mean come on, - Jack Jackson'

'Yeah man, my father was named Jack and my Mother thought it best we keep it simple" Jack's dark complexion brightened up with a smirk in the low moonlight.

'Oh shit I think I got a smile out of you, didn't I? I knew there was a human being underneath all that seriousness'

'Congratulations Jack Jackson, now let's find these missing children, so I can return to my woman and my canvases, and you can return to... well where are you living my friend?'

'I'm holed up in some central hotel near the Kremlin for a few months at least'

Max stopped the car at a lay-by on the approach to the woods.

`Good to meet you Jack Jackson' the men shook hands firmly, now let's go find these missing children. We sent out the scouting parties out a few hours ago, so far nothing has come up'

The car's intercom suddenly rang buzzed in - 'Sir we have found something, not sure if I know what it is, but it's something'

'Right here we go Jack' 'Right you are Max'

And the two friends went out into the dark together.

INNOCENCE LOST

My name is Alexey Petrovich and this is my new online blog which I entrust to whomever may read it. I have met the dark aspect incarnate in my work to rid the world of evil and this man has a name - that name is Alexander Grevich.

As I write here I present to you my thoughts on this man, though I can barely use that word in reference to him, as he is more of a monster than man, more demon than human, a man possessed of such evil that the very thought of him stops me from sleeping.

I have wandered now into the monastery to the Far East known as Vorkutlag, in search of answers from Malush and so it was upon one fateful night that I sat with the shamans of the Steppes and took the sacred Mushrooms they offered to me.

All my life I wanted to believe in the best in people, to see the good that lay beneath whatever earthly sins and troubles they may have been involved in.

I heard a tale of the great ship that the Temple of Malush was funding, a spaceship to explore further into space past the early Martian colonies the US had managed to install in the year 2065. We were promised that if we would donate enough circuits, enough wires through acts of penance and bargaining that we may be selected for the crew on this mad voyage into the depths of space, and it was there that my madness began, my lust for eternity.

My Adept duties were just one part of that journey that I wish to take to the stars, into the emptiness of space, and I knew Malush was the God who would take us there, as the great Mantor had shown us in his golden sacrifice, the man who did not destroy the world - bless that man, above all, still I speak his name in glory, although knowledge of the monster has blighted his light, he still shines above in the heavens.

What could create such a monster? How can such malevolence creep into the human soul? How and why does Malush the great allow for such evil in this world? All my faith is shaken to the core, and I now hastily scribble down this message in the vain hope that someone out there, perhaps a private detective or an agent of the law may find it and that it may aid in their investigation. I have studied several scientific books and I am fairly certain that we are dealing with a psychopath of the highest order, I have alas no evidence to back up my intuitions but if they speak truth in any regard it is this - Alexander Grevich's mind has been so twisted and gnarled, that perhaps it were best he was to be taken from this Earth.

I know it is wrong to kill, but in his case I think Malush may look the other way.

Please if any detectives pick up the case please contact me here at the retreat where I have gone to unpack my nerves, and to find peace. I enclose my address in the attachments.

Yours sincerely Alexey 'Maximo, it's Peter here, the techs found something that we would like you to look at when you return' 'Right you are' Max replied coolly as he and Jack trudged through the snow in the night towards the gathering police squad.

'Sergeant I am Detective Max and this is Detective Jack Jackson from the United States on a transfer program. Can you give me a quick low down on the current situation, what did you find?'

'I think it is best you take a look sir, but please prepare your stomach, it's not a pleasant sight to look upon for too long'

'If it's bad unfortunately that is our job, come on take us to the crime scene'

'Yes detective of course'

Max steps became slow and steady as he slowed his breath and breathed slowly through his nostrils, as Jack simply nodded, and they headed through the dimly lit woods to the scene of a large tree with a crouched figure kneeling at the base of it.

'Victim is female'

'Age, probably 13 or 14 years old'

'Painted red with some manner of paint, send it to forensics and mark that'

'Signs of trauma on the neck and a slash mark across the neck — cause of death seems to be a violent slashing of the throat, probably done with a knife'

;Her eyes are covered with a black bandage of some sort and lacerations are inflicted upon her body, on the back, the front and her legs;

'This is a goodman savage at work' Jack Mumbled

"You're telling me Jack, ok forensics we need to get blood samples. DNA swabs, and guys please you are relieved, please step away from the scene, this is our mess to clean up now".

'How can you stand to look at her, poor thing'

'It's our job to catch these kinds of monsters, now move along Sergeant and get back to your family if you got one, that goes for all you guys, we just need forensics to stay. Me and Jack are going to do a forensic scan of the area, please interview anyone in a 5-mile radius and ask them if they saw anything unusual before this poor girl was murdered, me and Jack will speak to the family tomorrow, you've done brilliantly gentleman now take it easy and let the professionals do their grim work for the evening"

Jack and Max looked at each other with eyes of sadness.

'These cases are the fucking worse' - they didn't need to say it, they just read it in each other's eyes as they started the long drive back silently to the Police headquarters. 'So this Alexey Petrovich, seems a big unhinged hey?'

"He's innocent Peter"

'We can't be too damn sure" I am sending you out to talk to him next week, first thing Monday Max, don't let me down'

'Of that you have my guarantee, there is too much at stake now'

Peter nodded at Max who headed to his new office and sat down at his computer, a slightly battered old thing and booted up the message to analyse it further.

'He is clearly afraid of this man, something in him stirs difficult feelings, but we shouldn't jump to any conclusions' thought Max as he shifted through the paragraphs.

'His personality indicates Alexey Petrovich to be an honest and good man dedicated to service, at least on the surface, He holds no past criminal records save for a few minor offences in his youth — some minor drug charges but hey I'd be a hypocrite if I didn't understand that at least' Max chuckled, a buzz on Max's phone, it was Julia calling.

'Ahh Hello Julia'

'Hey Max, how is it going?'

'I don't want to tell you this, but we found one'

'Oh Malush no, please Malush no'

'You are an Adept of the Machine God?'

'How can you say that at a time like this, a child is, is ...'

'Dead'

'Fucking bastard, you find who did this Max, you find who did this and you make them pay, you hear me!'

'I hear you loud and clear, lets see each other this weekend, I have a long week ahead of me, please if you could bring me some coffee I would appreciate it my love'

'You are a good man.'

'I know, I know I am, I await our warm embrace my love, I will get you flowers when next we meet'

'And we lay some at the grave of the girl?'

'And we lay some at the grave of the girl.'

They both paused for a moment in the solemn silence that descended;

'It is at times like this I need art, as an escape, an escape from the mundane horror of it all' Max voice broke slightly on the phone as he said the words.

'I'll be seeing you on the Eternal ship soon enough, stay strong my love, I love you'

Julia put down the phone, and Max grimaced, missing her touch more intensely now, missing the warm stroke of her hand on his sad face, contorted at what he must now face.

EVIL INCARNATE?

Today is my first journal in the case of "Who is Mantor's Nemesis? I write here at my desk with an impossible task before me, to try and understand the mind of a deranged human being, full of violence, full of fear - a decaying bully.

I assume the killer must be a man, not a woman who I cannot imagine would be capable of enacting such savage violence upon an innocent child, this bears the mark of a serial killer in its ritual, as it seems pattern based, and in this journal I shall attempt to think about the motivations behind the ritual.

This man, and I assume it is a man, has I imagine a fixation on his Mother as a negative anima figure, he resents his mother to the point of pure malevolent hatred, he collects his victims as trophies to show to her, to seek her approval always. This is indicated by the slashing of the throat which implies a will to cut off the victims source of life - the lungs. This indicates that the suspect had some deep trauma from his youth, which he has chosen to enact on others in return.

The colour red indicates the start of something, perhaps he sees what he is doing as art.

What he is doing could not be further from art.

In the suspects mind, what he is doing is serving his mother, perhaps the overattachment to a Mother figure indicates a homosexual, though I doubt that what we are dealing with here is quite so simple, and I would recommend that we don't pursue such leads based on sexual orientation alone, as it seems too obvious and reductive. Gay men are generally comfortable with their sexuality, and no more or less capable of such homicidal violence in general like anyone else, so it doesn't seem relevant, no, it is not at all.

This was much more deeper than that, perhaps involving a ritual cross dressing?

Again it goes much deeper I feel somehow. This is ritual, and though many of the various occult books I have consulted in the past explore the relationship between sex and the occult, this is some much deeper drive than sex alone.

Unfortunately we are certainly dealing with a chronic child abuser of the utmost severity given the young age of many of the victims. We will need to look into the old archives post-war for any men accused of sexual offences. I think these are the crimes of an older or middle aged man of medium or strong build, as indicated by that blade cut to the throat - so I will recommend that the team start by looking for a male, past the age of 30 with a prior conviction for molestation or rape convictions, possibly a juvenile delinquent.

We are dealing with a possible serial killer of the utmost savagery here ladies and gentlemen, let's engage our brains and get out there and find this maniac, thank you.

Max sighed and looked out his office windows as he completed his debrief to his small team of detectives, time to visit Julia and Kristian on the Eternal ship again. The fear was palpable in the air as Max walked out of his office and into the dark unforgiving night. ;See you later Max; shouted Jack from down the corridor

'Later, Jack' Max shouted to Jack Jackson, himself buried in books at this desk as Max flew from the Moscow Police HQ.

A buzz on the flats intercom echoed out through the eternal ship as Max waited outside in the cold, the snowflakes dropping down on his head from above and melting into his ushanka, wetting his hair slightly. 'Ahh you are here, at last, come in'

Max walked in the door into the Eternal Ship, drawings adorning the walls as in the corridor he spotted a small portrait of two figures smiling and looking deep into his eyes. He began to get lost in the picture, it had a swirling blue background and the two figures were painted in a bright crimson red.

'He is quite the artist isn't he' Julia said smiling at Max and breaking his trance.

'Indeed, he is very talented, very recklessly expressionist!'

Julia and Max laughed out loud, 'Let's have a coffee and ask Kristian about it" Max nodded and entered the kitchen, again adorned with artwork.

'Hello' Kristian said, a shy young boy of probably the age of 8 looked at Max as he froze, still cold from the -15 weather outside.

'Hello young artist! Your Mother has told me much about you, and I am glad to meet a fellow traveller!" Max said, extending out his hand to the young boy, who after a brief moment extended out his own and shook it before running to his room to play with his charcoal. Julia looked at Max with sudden eyes of concern as the worry of the killer at large descended on the room.

'I wrote you a poem Max, I hope it will help you, to aid you in your investigation when it becomes emotionally tough.'

Max softly embraced Julia and whispered in her ear 'Don't worry, I will find him, and when I do, he will face justice' Julia's hair prickled as he whispered in her ear, and he kissed her on the neck with loving attention and care. 'I know' she said looking at him with her deep set eyes 'I know you will, because we must protect the young ones, if that monster ever found Kristian, well there are no words for what I would do to the man who did it"

'It will never come to that, I am the captain of this ship, and none shall pollute its corridors!' said Max, as he thought of the killer, and a tremble went down his spine.

'Let's go to the art room my love, I have many things to show you'

Julia put the poem into Max's hand, and he began to read it slowly in the kitchen as she ran to the art room He is the Great Owl,

His hoots. It's ravenous amongst the clouds.

Protects and provides;'

He is the great Owl

He keeps guard

My tears shall not swell his growing -

In my heart.

'I am the great owl, wise, and I will guard this ship with my life' Max promised to the Ship as his eyes looked above, and he became lost in daydreaming.

'Come on Max, I'm waiting and anxious to paint'

'Coming dear' and with that Max ran down the small staircase to her studio. 'Here is the painting I am working on at the minute - it's a sea scene as you can see, I went to the port city of Kaliningrad and painted it from life, what do you think Max, oh do make sure to tell me the truth' 'It's good, great actually, you have a precise handling of brushstrokes, texture and form. I feel as if I am warmed by it, I can feel the heat of the sun, for now so distant in time, at present.' Max responded with his honest critique which came from his heart as well as his head.

Julia smiled, 'So now do you need a lady to paint perchance?'

Max's mischievous grin returned 'Oh I thought you would never ask, disrobe, and I shall paint you as I see you in my mind, nude to the eye, nude to my soul.'

Max had before him a pallet and many tubes of paint, an entire rainbow of primary colours lay before him, blue of course must be used, but he wondered about the background colour? Red? No too dramatic, too angry, I must use a complimentary colour like yellow I think, and also it will help to capture the evening glow of the fading light.

'So Max, paint me like one of your French girls hey?' Julia said with a sly grin 'But tell me dear boy, how do I know you don't have a girl at every port?'

'I don't, believe me you have not seen the state of my studio yet!' and with that terrible confession Max made his first mark on the canvas before him as Julia began to take down her dress and settled on the bed, her arse wobbling before Max's eyes like some long forgotten glory, her pert breasts seeming to glisten before him as she lay before her half mad Artist lover.

'Hmm' thought Max as he examined the beauty before him 'I really do need to get this one right, this is going to be the toughest case of all - to make sure that I portray her radiant beauty so that it pleases her, and she will know my heart of hearts in an instant upon seeing it on the canvas threads'

'Go on my love, don't leave a lady waiting' she giggled resplendent on the bed with her blue hair seeming to glow in the dim yellow light of the studio.

Max began by sketching out the surroundings around her in pencil so as to get an idea of how to frame her body, roughly sketching out the composition of her surroundings before he framed off the rough area where her body laid, lying down and looking above at the ceiling.

"Make me look pretty Max" Max just grinned at her and rolled his eyes slightly with a quiet smile before he began to draw the contours of her body, accentuating and erotic, like Matisse would've done, or perhaps Picasso when painting one of his many conquests, but no, she was more like Modigliani's Jeanne to him, though he tried to force the idea out of his head, given the particularly tragic ending that had haunted their tragic romance. This painting had to be a painting of her by him, not a pale imitation of the great artists of the past, and so it was that he began on his work, going into a trance like state.

Several hours passed and Julia began to get a little cranky 'Max I'm getting stiff I think I need a break, would you like a cup of tea?'

Max was still engrossed in his work

'Tea dear!' said Julia with a tone of bemusement 'Ahh yes, time for a break I suppose' he was almost finished, just another 30 minutes and she would be there on the threads — looking back at them both, frozen in time — the first gift given to the Eternal Ship. Julia came in covered in her dressing gown with a warm mug of tea and handed it to Max as he prepared to paint again, and she relaxed back into her original position on the bed. 'Brilliant, you are a natural Julia' Max smiled as he returned to the window of his painting and began the process of slowly tying off the last parts of the painting in earnest. 'So Max' Julia interjected 'How is the case going?' a look of concern etching her face.

'Please not right now Julia'

'Why not?'

'I like to keep work and pleasure separate, this for me is pure pleasure, and escape into the senses, a lounging in the sensuality of paint and canvas, out there in the world though I must be tough, and make my soul brittle against the horrors I am forced to confront, this is my only escape"

A look of distant sadness clouded his eyes

'I am sorry, I will return to my rest my dear Maximo'

But the thought was now in his head and he began to think about the significance of the paint used again as he applied a few careful brushstrokes to the breast, his subtle brush now worn out from the pouring expressionism of before.

'Why there?' he thought aloud suddenly without realising it

'Pardon Max?'

'Oh nothing, I'm just thinking aloud'

'Why would the killer slash the throat so brutally? Could it be he feels silenced somehow and these killings are his outlet?

Perhaps it's an externalisation of his own fear? Fear of himself and perhaps guilt? That indeed might be a line of inquiry considering the crime we think may lie in his past.... Or maybe a way of expressing rage at women and girls in general, but what lies behind that fear? Is this man a virgin? Haunted by impotence maybe? A violent lashing out at society perhaps?

'Max! Julia shouted suddenly 'Max, you're spilling paint on the floor!'

'Ahh, oh sorry I was lost in thought' as Max's brush dripped acrylic paint on the floor of the carpet. 'It's ok, it's my fault I should have put down newspaper as I usually do, here you go here is a copy of the Moscow Times, only thing it's good for these days anyway haha'

Max took the newspaper and unfurled it quickly catching a glimpse of the front page news The Cult of Mansu announces it is almost ready for its first manned mission into the cosmos,

'Hmm interesting' thought Max 'So they already managed to do it finally, all those donations may have not been for nought after all'

Red

The colour flashed before his eyes suddenly as he entered a trance state of sorts as his visually linguistic imagination began to fire off a free association of phrases 'Red like fire, red like burning, red like passion, red like heart, red like blood,

red like lust, red like love, red like, red revolution, red institu-
tion…, red like'
    'Paint.'

THE MONK'S RETREAT

It was Wednesday and the slow and ponderous train journey to Alexey's retreat was finally drawing to a close, as Maximo and Jack exited the ancient soviet era train that screeched to a halt at their final stop. It was Vorkutlag, one of the largest labour camps of the Soviet era, which now during the reformation had been converted into a retreat for lost souls, or those who needed respite from the harshness of the world.

It was ran by a Orthodox Priest named Olga, who beckoned them into its dimly lit chambers before they arrived at a medium-sized room adorned with paintings, seemingly random doodles and photographs arranged with wires connecting them and a gruff looking slightly lanky, dishevelled man staring out the window, gazing at the moon in the distance.

'Alexey I presume' Maximo said softly as he and Jack entered the room and Olga nodded and left the men to their work.

'Ahh yes that is me, and who may I ask are you? I have not received many visitors since my.. My, my retirement from Mantor's light...' he shivered slightly in the dark, as if someone had walked over his grave.

'We are from the police department of Moscow, and we picked up the note you left for us on your blog'

'Oh, thank Mansu, thank you Mantor, protector of us all' Alexey shouted, suddenly snapping out of his sullen sunken state "I had no idea anyone would actually pick it up, oh thank

you, than..' he was interrupted suddenly by Jack who interjected;

'We have questions, please sit down and we will see to it,
nothing to worry about Alexey merely a formality we believe'
Jack said as Maximo stroked his beard with intent, surveying
the body language and the tone of voice that the Priest used -
they had to suspect everyone.

  'Ok first things first we need to know why you are here, the
short version if you will' Maximo said as they drew up two
chairs across from Alexey who huddled at the window with a
nervous agitated look in his eye as if a feral rat cornered by
two hungry cats.

'Oh Mansu, Mansu, Mansu" Alexey began to sob, withdrawing
from the two men who eyed him with suspicion 'Where do I
begin, how did it begin.' a look of madness began consuming
him on his face as it contorted, as if talking to an invisible god
above.

;It was a crisis of Faith I assume; Maximo posited, looking at
Alexey with eyes of inquisition.
  'Oh it was much more than that I can assure you Officer, it
was service'

'Service to what?' Jack countered perceiving the unease of the
man's nerves collapsing in front of them.

'Why Mansu of course! Aha!' he giggled this time like a
demented infant with a sinister air of violent cunning.

'What is Mansu to you Alexey?' 'My master Officer, merely my
master'

'And how do you serve this Master of yours?' Maximo looked at the Priest with a look of stern silent anger now.

'Sacrifice Gentlemen, sacrifice'

Max's brow stiffened as he felt that same chill down his spine again and the air seemed to leave the room as both Jack and Max felt the tension building in the air, as Maximo starting to smile like a fool sick of sin, and his sinning. 'This could be him… perhaps I was wrong to presume such a seemingly innocent man could not be capable of such savage acts, I wonder how many others there are, I need to talk to Jack.

'Jack we need a moment alone, let's get someone to watch Alexey here for a moment, call Olga and tell her we need a moment to speak with her too, Alexey please do not move, or we will be forced to use force against you, do you under-stand?'

Alexey looked terrified and anxious like someone had sud-denly awakened him from a terrible dream; 'What? You cannot think that! You must not think that! No! No! No!'

Alexey began howling with despair and wailing, banging his head against the window before him, smashing the window pane into several pieces and cutting his forehead in the process.

'The fuck!' Jack shouted in disbelief as Alexey wept and began screaming like a toddler on the ground.

'Let's book him and take him back to HQ" Max said, a look of disgust etched on his face as he looked down at Alexey who wept in the fetal position before them.

"I think we might have a clear lead, lets clean up this mess and get this weird fucker back for questioning"

The two men called for Olga who entered the room coldly and looked at them both with a look of disgust in her eyes; "What the hell! What have you done to our client?! You don't do something like this to an Adept!"

'With the greatest of respect lady, we are the Police and we are on a murder case, so kindly..'
    Max got out his handcuffs and put them around Alexey's wrists' tightly,
    'Get out of the way.'

She was appalled and huffed off down the corridor with a haughty air of self-righteousness;
    'You will be hearing from our High Priest, Mansu and the children of Mantor do not look kindly on such intrusions into our order, and we are so close to the stars now, we need every adept we can get."

Jack retorted 'Well yeah, but we want our children safe, and we have sufficient reason to suspect that this man may be involved in this case, so let us out of here lady, so we can do our job.'

'Fine, but expect a call from our lawyers'
    'Cyka' whispered Max under his breath, 'cyka'.

'I hear you' Jack said as he looked at Max with concerned eyes..

Jack and Maximo acquired a police car from the local station nearby and began their long drive away from Vorkutlag with Alexey handcuffed in the back of the cab, unconscious for now with closed eyes staring into the empty void.

'So what do you think is going on here Max?' Jack looked at his partner, calculating at the wheel with a stern hard expression on his face as they drove on tyet another snow covered road in the darkness of the night.

'We need to press him for more information, that much is clear to me, well perhaps we have our man, but we must be sure, we must connect all the dots together to get a fuller picture, I would say he shows sign of psychopathy or at least a profound disturbance – the talk of sacrifice is of course for concern, but why write to us, why reach out?'

'An inner desire to be caught perhaps" interjected Jack 'A guilt or inner conscience kicking in?' 'Perhaps Jack, many of these ritualistic killers can be so driven and debased that they want to gaud us, some even have shown remorse in the past... perhaps we can reach the human in him if he is guilty. Either way we need to push him for as much information as possible, we need to establish motivations, and develop a psychological profile of him, we can keep him in for questioning for a few days, let's extract as much as we can in the time we have but make no assumptions yet, this could yet be a red herring, we can assume nothing, we need to make sure our case is strong and any evidence we can obtain is concrete.'

Maximo looked at his partner, who looked a little nervous in his seat.

'It rattled you a little didn't it Jack, the way he just banged his head into the glass, such a wilful disregard for his own life, such self-destructive behaviour. It is always unsettling dealing with such men, damaged from the harshness of this world.

Always remember one thing though Jack, we serve but one master and that master is the truth, truth and justice'

'I suppose you are right Max, I've dealt with a few homicide cases before back in the states, but mostly gang related cases, much more black and white, less horrific and ritualistic in nature.'

'You will get used to it' Max said as they continued along the snow driven road as Max rang into the local precinct to obtain permission for a formal recorded interview at the local station in Vorkuta

'Vorkuta Police HQ, how can we help?'

'Greetings Vorkuta HQ, this is Maximo Zinoev of the Moscow police department, we have apprehended a suspect in a homicide case and would like to formally request an interview room and facilities to interview a suspect as part of ongoing investigation, my name is Maximo Zinoev, badge number is 04532, and I am with my partner Jack Jackson badge number 03453 a contract transfer in from the United States. Please confirm the above, and we will be with you in 40 minutes driving from the Vorkutlag rehabilitation centre."
    'Ok Detectives, I am checking in with the commissioner now, and you can expect confirmation in 20 mins, keep safe out there, it's a particularity stormy night, confirmation will arrive via your vehicles HUD soon, good night'

'That's it then' thought Max, time to mentally prepare as he and Jack sped off towards the nearby station to begin their further probing, the stakes now unquestionably getting higher.

A ping on the HUD as the police station confirmed the use of their facilities.

'Here we go' thought Max as they drove on in the night.

WHO IS MANTOR'S NEMESIS?

The two detectives pulled into the Vorkuta Police HQ, an austere brutalist building in severe disrepair. Like most of the police in Russia, the reformation was a slow process and the state was still modernising slowly, and as with many government facilities Vorkuta Police HQ ran on a shoestring budget from the central councils, themselves forced to allocate based on need.

The priest began to wake up from his rest, he was restrained with handcuffs in the back of the police vehicle.

"He's coming round" Jack Jackson said to Maximo in the front of the car as the Priest's eyes began slowly opening in the gloomy police car park, as heavy snowfall pounded down on them from above and a harsh wind howled outside. "Where are we? Where am I?" Alexey blurted out as he came into fuller consciousness, his eyes stinging as passing lights flooded his vision.

'We are going to Vortuka Police HQ to question you further Alexey, please comply with us in all and anything we ask you, and we can sort this mess out once and for all' Max answered as he looked for a parking space in the dimly lit police car park, pulling into a clear spot in the corner, "You cannot seriously think I am behind such monstrous crimes" protested Alexey as he grimaced with the dry blood on his face.

'Like I said Alexey we simply need to ask you some questions, comply and tell the truth, that is all we ask of you'

'Fine, I want this man caught just as much as you do, of that I can assure you officers'

Max parked the car as Jack Jackson escorted Alexey, hand-cuffed to him, into the large concrete building, as they arrived at the Police HQ's reception.

'Maximo Zinov and Jack Jackson reporting' said Max as they signed in to reception to get access to the interview room and entered the cold, sterile room with a single table and chair ready for the suspect, and two chairs and a recording unit setup for the detectives to do their interrogation. Jack escorted Alexey to his chair and handcuffed him to the table as the two detectives sat down and pressed record on the tape recorder.

"So Alexey, this is a formal notice for the record that we are now recording this interview on the 20th November 2080, we just want to ask you several questions to determine your location on several dates to aid in an ongoing investigation, do you understand?"

Alexey looked distant, but nodded to the two men who faced him now as Max began his line of questioning "So Alexey on the evening of the 15th of November can you give me a description of your whereabouts on that night at roughly 8pm?"

"I can indeed officer, I had just booked my train journey to Vartuka with my intention to leave for the retreat, due to a crisis of faith"

'And what precipitated this crisis of Faith Alexey? Can you provide some evidence for us of this journey? A train ticket, we will of course check your sign in details with the retreat to corroborate your claims'

'It is no claim detectives, it is the truth! I had to get out of Moscow, my conscience was playing havoc with my nerves…'

'So you had a guilty conscious' Jack butted in 'What did you feel guilty about?'

'It was as I said a crisis of faith'

'Again I ask you, what prompted this 'crisis of faith' 'Evil' Alexey responded nervously, visibly agitated 'Evil? What evil?"

Max inquired, his eyes narrowing as he analysed Alexey's body language as he squirmed in his chair looking suddenly uncomfortable. 'Have to keep pushing him just the right amount' he thought to himself.

'So Detectives it is time I must make my confession' he sighed as the two detectives suddenly stiffened up in their chairs 'You are responsible for some evil? And your conscience is guilty?' Max pressed him further 'Alas no officers, if only it were that simple, my soul would surely be damned of course, it is more that I let such evil pass, and though I warned the authorities , I worry that it may yet be stalking the streets of Moscow.... that evil is the man Alexander Grevich!"

Max and Jack looked at each other suddenly and leaned forward together 'Who is Alexander Grevich? Who is Mantor's nemesis' Max's voice began to rise as he became impatient with the Priest and his riddles. 'This is an important matter Adept, tell us everything you know!'

'I was assigned to this man Alexander Grevich but a month ago by the cult of Mansu, he seemed a troubled man, and the welfare office were at their wits end trying to reform him for assigned work, and so as often is the case they thought he may be of use to our order as a missionary, to reform both his mind and to put his corrupt soul on some path of redemption. I visited his residence on the 10th November to assess his suitability, but .... But"

'But what?' Max pushed him for more information 'I immediately felt a negative presence around this man, like a black hole was sucking all the light out the room when he entered, he is a man in his early forties, but he lives still with his Mother in Moscow who I felt exerted some sort of bizarre pull on him, I could feel the resentment he had towards his mother, but there was more than that. There was some malevolence in that room too, truly evil malevolent energy.'

'We need more than this' Jack whispered in Max's ear as Alexey continued his monologue,

'This is all speculation, it could even be a strategy to sideline us'

'Ok we hear you Alexey, this man disturbed you, but how can we be expected to...'

Suddenly Alexey was cut off as his phone began to buzz, it was Moscow HQ phoning in,

'A minute please, Jack please keep an eye on Alexey'

Max went out of the interview room to take the call

'There has been another one Max, another victim was found on the outskirts of Moscow this afternoon, time of death estimated as a few days ago, we need you both in Moscow" Peter's solemn voice echoed down the phone

'I am sorry to hear it, we are making some progress with the Adept, and we will escort him to Moscow once we have tied off some loose ends, dammit, I was hoping we may have had the bastard!' Max shouted in despair down the phone.

'You'll get your guy, let's debrief after you finished you interview at Vartuka and then book you on a flight from the airport ASAP.'

'Yes Captain, thank you for the update' Max's nerves felt that chill again 'not another one'

'I was so foolish to hope that perhaps its was a one off, it is never the way with such monsters, time to tie off the loose ends here and return to Moscow'

VOYAGE TO THE VOID

'The hour draws closer Mansu, surely I have given enough now' spluttered Alexander as he flailed in his dim basement surrounded by flesh and wire. "Soon Mansu soon, we will ascend to the stars, in our eternal ship! All the dolls will rise up and..."

Alexander paused suddenly "will dance amongst the dust of the cosmos" He began to laugh maniacally in fits of obscene ecstasy, surrounded by his sightless dolls whose dead eyes stared blankly at him, curated like some obscene inversion of an art exhibition. "And you will lead the parade!" Alexander giggled pointing at the corpse of his Mother, her cadaver now mutilated beyond recognition, with a collage of circuits haphazardly forced into parts of her now putrid flesh. Alexander ran to his console giggling still like a demented infant in the grim, dimly lit basement and headed to his console as he began typing on its screen, letters burning blue on the screen before him.

'Will Mansu have me now?' He wondered.

Application to the Cult of Mansu's inaugural space mission

Role: Maintenance Worker Salary: Board and Basic pay of 300 Rubles per hour

Description: Voyage into the unknown with the followers of Mansu, as the spiritual warriors of Mantor aim to follow his intrepid spirit. We will be engaging in a resource collection mission to aid our growing movement and so that Mantor's spirit may rise again - The light of Mansu will reach to the stars! As a maintenance worker you will be responsible for basic ship maintenance along with a team of other recruits. Basic training will be provided.

Alexander laughed again and pressed submit to complete his application. It was the afternoon of the 22nd of November and Maximo and Jack were sitting in Peter's office exploring their options.

'Well officers, where are we at now with this case?'

'We interviewed the Adept, and we need to urgently find this man Alexander Grevich'

"And what's your assessment of this Priest, a possible suspect?' Peter asked lighting his cigar 'It's possible, perhaps all this talk of this Grevich is just a decoy, something to take us off his trail, but his statements do line up, and he was with us when the further killings took place so he has a tight alibi for the latest murders.'

Peter nodded "Please catch up with forensics, and find this man Grevich, we need to tie this one up lads, we've lost too many already, and the disquiet is growing on the streets.'

Maximo and Jack were heading to the forensics lab when suddenly Max received a buzz on his phone. How are you Max? I am worried the message glared like a bright light on his phone. 'I will return to you soon my love' thought Max as he and Jack walked briskly to their grim but necessary work.
'Once more with the slashing of the neck, did the team pick up anything more of interest, any DNA results yet?" Jack asked the young forensic scientist standing before him nervously shuffling. 'No, I'm afraid not officer, it appears who ever is doing this, knows how to cover their tracks'

'This is a waste of time' Max was grumpy

'We need to look up this Grevich as soon as possible, let's get to it Jack, search for all males named Alexander Grevich in the Moscow area, filter for delinquents with period convictions, this may well be an open and shut case I suspect.'

'Hopefully so' nodded Jack as the two men nodded to the scientist, gathered his documents and left the forensics area. Jack booted up his computer monitor which glowed green as a list of records pinged up in front of him, and he entered the password to access the government's citizens database Search for : Grevich, Alexander Sex: Male

Age: 18 - 55

Filter for : Prior convictions

"Let's get this list printed out and cross reference with the Priest, time is of the essence Jack" Max was getting agitated

'It will never stop chilling me to the bones, all the faces frozen in their death masks, so much horror, and for what? Hubris, delusion, all death…"

"Ok Max I have it, let's talk to the Priest"

The two detectives walked into the cell that Alexey was now housed in, a medium-sized room with a small barred window as they edged the door open and went inside.

'Alexey, we hope you are ready for some further question-ing' Max slammed down the list that Jack had printed off down on the small table to his left. 'We have produced a list of all the men named Alexander Grevich in the Moscow area, we are going to take you out to the place where you said he lived with his Mother and if we get a positive match for a man on this list, it will help us form a bigger picture of what is going on here, do you understand?'

'Yes of course officers, I can take you there and will do all that you ask of me, I want him caught as much as you do, I can assure you" the Adept said nodding and rocking a bit in the corner.

'Mansu can forgive much, but for Alexander, it is too late, he is truly lost to the void, he must have voyaged far too deep into the darkness that lies dormant in every man.'

'Ok Alexey enough with the philosophy, we have to go now' said Max as they escorted the half mad Priest from his cell and out into another sombre night of work. 'Why haven't they responded yet? What to do in the meantime I wonder, shall I play with them Mantor?'

Mantor looked down from the portrait before him, candlelight lighting his anointed face as it glowed in the darkness of the Clown's void, and suddenly began to speak in hushed tones to his servant. 'Play my child, play. Life, death, all is eternal here in the depths of the void, deep in the depths of our Eternal Ship"

The clown sniggered as he returned to his haunted circle in the dark.

'So this is the place Alexey?' they had pulled up to the small residential cottage on the outskirts of the Southside of Moscow, a rickety place that Max felt had an ominous feeling of decay to it as he felt the all too familiar shiver down his spine.

"This is the place Officers"

'Ok Jack you watch the Adept, I'm going to knock on, you have your pistol Jack, first sign of any trouble or if I radio in you get me some cover and don't let that goddamn priest out of your sight until he is secularly handcuffed, understood?'

Jack nodded as he secured the Priest in handcuffs and kept watch over the car, as Max slowly approached the half ruined cottage with trepidation in his steps.

'This place looks like it hasn't had the grass cut for a decade, very little sign of life on the outside that is for sure' Max thought as he gripped his gun tightly, anticipating anything, and feeling for the first time on this case, the nervous rising of anxiety from deep his gut, as he approached the worn wooden door and rang the old doorbell on the right-hand side.

The silence before the storm perhaps? The silence was deafening as he waited at the door, he had to take this one slowly, no point rushing in guns blazing, it would only destroy the case, every lead had to be investigated so that the case would be as strong as possible, if they had found the monster at last,

'No answer, I'm going in' Max radioed into Jack 'Roger that,let me know if you need backup'

Max kicked at the old door frame, it took a few solid kicks to the lock before it swung upon to reveal the house within, and he entered. 'Police! We are here for Alexander Grevich!' he bellowed as he entered the dark dull interior.

'Police, if anyone is here show yourself now'

He repeated again as he drew his gun from its holder and aimed it before him, in case of a sudden attack. There was no reply, and not a sound could be heard.

'Perhaps that mad Priest is having us on, goddammit I hope this isn't another goddamn dead end' Max grabbed his radio to update Jack 'Seems that no-one is home, at least we got a goddamn search warrant, let's do a scan and search, get in here Jack let's do a thorough search for anything we can find.'

'I really long for the Eternal ship, to be one with my love again, to relax and be far from all this, all this death and despair, thank God I have my little corner of paradise' thought Max before he suddenly stiffened thinking he heard a faint sound from below, something that sounded like a loud snigger followed by clattering. "Police! Hands up!" He shouted as he raised his pistol in the dark, and quickly switched on the light switch in the hallway. Max thought it best to wait for Jack to arrive before proceeding.

'Get in here Jack, I heard something'

'I'm here Jack appeared by his side with his pistol drawn at mid-level, what did you hear Max?'

'I am sure I heard a clattering sound and what sounded like laughter coming from somewhere below, let's check if there is a basement in the building, you cover me you hear'

'That I will Max, just take it slow'

Max scanned the area with his eyes, as Jack turned on more lights to reveal portraits of Mantor pinned to every wall in the house, and a collection of bizarre ornaments on every shelf.

'Whoever this Grevich is, it seems he is a bit of a hoarder to say the least' Jack chuckled. 'Shhhh Jack, for fuck's sake' Max grimaced with annoyance, as he spotted a staircase going downwards in the far end of the living room. 'Alright Max I'm sorry my friend, now you just watch your step going down there, I'll spot you on the way down'

And with that Max descended into the deep void of the Clown of Mansu's madness.

THE DEPTHS OF THE BLACKHOLE

'Alexander Grevich! Open up now!' the sweat beads were slowly forming on Max's head as Jack covered him from behind, sweat beads forming on his forehead in the cold from nerves, he had been here before, and invariably he would be here again, protecting the world from it's most depraved children.

There was silence, terrible silence.

'Jack, you said you had some technical experience, check that lock would you and let's get into this fucking basement, Christ the stink, clammy ageing hands' Max clutched his pistol. Jack nodded and took out a mobile device.

'Here's hoping my Nephew is quite the whizz he always boasts about' Jack whispered as he tampered with the door's lock, as cryptic symbols began to whirl around on the screen like a carousel of digital angels circling limbo, here to save the lost children.

The monitor was glowing green and burning into Jack's eyes as he observed the patterns before him looking for the lock

'1, 2,3 Max...' Jack looked to his partner 'Get ready and... yeah damn that Motherfuckers smart' a look of satisfaction on Jack's face,

Max stiffened up as the silence descended, a silence as long as a death gasp in his mind, as they prepared to enter the limbo of Mansu.

'Thank God they sent someone capable at last, the last American I was partnered with was far too soft for this line of work, the war case.'

The two men entered the room which was piled high with debris from every conceivable angle, the stench of decay and rot overwhelming as the two men covered their faces with their long coats and tried not to gag.

'I have a feeling we have our man Jack, Alexander Grevich!' Max shouted as loud as his lungs would allow him.

Suddenly a lone monitor in the distance began to boot up and a grainy video began to play, it was degraded purposefully, a crouched hooded figure sat in an empty room began to speak with a dull voice that sounded like it was half dead.

'Have you come for me at last Mantor? Come to take me to the skies above? I have been saving all my circuits for you'

The voice shook a little

'Saving all the dolls I can find, all ornaments of course, all for you Mantor, for Mansu and the Gods above, why worry about the flesh when your dark spirit has shown me a world beyond the flesh, mere disposable vessels!"

'Max!' a sudden violent flash from the door on the far side of the room as a bullet flew past Max's right side striking him hard in the shoulder As he fell to the floor with a thud, the impact of the bullet propelling him to the floor, and his pulse began racing'

'Jack! Get him!' Max was able to sputter out though the pain as Max saw the Monster before him — a gaunt looking man with lank long hair, as thin as a scarecrow, with eyes that looked more like black holes sucking all the light out of the room, Max's vision was blurred in the darkness as the pain entered his body.

Jack rose his pistol and fired a single shot, and then there was silence.

'You Sick Fuck!' Jack screamed at the man in the chair with disgust, as Alexander Grevich the man sat before them tied to a worn old metal chair, which had the markings of rust around it, the mark of decay which haunted this entire cursed place.

'Don't fuck him up Jack, we'll do that in the courts' Max said as he limped into the room and touched his partner on the back

'You will see space Alexander, it is all you will see forever, you will be alone forever in the darkest hole we can find for you, and their souls will be free' Max looked into the room beyond where the stench emanated from

'And they will be your captors, 'dolls' you called them? They are angels, you fool!' he spat as Jack led the monster out of his temporary cage to the infinite one he would eek out the rest of his sad existence in,

Alexander said nothing, a thousand yard stare etched on his face as if frozen in time.

Max entered the dolls chamber and grabbing a cloth from the side, ripped it into several pieces to give the children within a safe passage to the next life, pennies for the ferryman. As he heard the car driving off into the distance, he sat down in the rusting chair as silent tears welled in his eyes and taking out his camera took photographic evidence for the forensics team before patching up the hole in his shoulder with the cloth he had picked up in this hellhole..

'In the eternal ship, you will all be free, Of this I promise you, you Angels.'

His dark figure punctuated the darkness, as distant lights shone through the ruined cottage.

A silent prayer to eternity. A promise to the families, all the reasons he had taken the case, the work was done, and justice would be finally be served.

THE OTHER SIDE

Alexey finished his story and looked out with sad old eyes at the children who gathered before him sat in silent contemplation as the old man told his tale. He had embellished all the details of course, made it more fantastical so as to protect them from the simple, terrible truth—some men are just bad, and sometimes men have to do questionable things to protect them.

'Do we understand the morale of this tale?' he intoned to his students

'Don't be a bad person'

'Yes that is a given' chuckled Alexey to Konstantin.

'But what of the deeper truth children, the bones under the skin?'

'Love' a small girl who had been hiding in the background said

'Love conquers all, and no matter how dark the darkest night may be, however hard the snow may fall there is always someone who will endure the pain to make the most of the worst, the truth of it, is that it about hope'

Alexey smiled at the intelligent young girl, a little older than the others with golden hair and an impish moon like face wearing small glasses, looking out like she lived somewhere between worlds.

'And what of Maximo and Julia?' she enquired quizzically.

'They are still with us in spirit child, looking at us still through these portals! Art! The portal to the world before our own, and they are the reason I created our own group of budding artists, as penance for not catching a demon before it was too late. A way for the angels to live on and never fade out from our view, see Max even painted a portrait for each one, pored the rest of his life over each one lost to the dark, his penance for not saving them from dead earth they lay them in.'

The small girl looked at Alexey, who began to shiver a little from his haunted memories of Vartuka, she looked deeply into his eyes as a small wry smile formed on her face as she saw who Alexey she could see was–an innocent man who did the right thing, not a warrior but a good man nonetheless.

The girl's name was Marsha Zinoev and Maximo's dream had come true.

DIARY ENTRY

This is the diary of Marsha Zinoev, I am aged 12, and I live in Moscow, Russia.

My Mother and Father told me something I didn't know before today, apparently my Grandmother and Father were once great artists in Moscow, which is strange because today my art teacher was telling me a strange story about a terrible monster and two artists, one of whom was a detective! An Artist and a Detective! Can you imagine such a strange mix! Maybe there is a connection?

I will have to refer to my books to find out more, I will talk to my Mum and try and get here to take me to the library, she always talks about how her Father used to force her to the library all the time, but it's my favourite place in the world.

I suppose I am writing this letter to my future self, so I would just like to say—don't worry about seeming odd or strange to the world, I mean you could be an artist or a detective or both, but if you love people for what they are, and make sure that you do right by them, love will always find a way, I guess it did for Max and Julia, I wish I had known them when they were younger.

Alas my parents say they are gone for now, long departed to an Island somewhere to the west, settled forever in their enteral ship in the stars. I think they said it's called it retirement?

Well anyway, to my future self and anyone who reads this

Love and truth will find a way.
Marsha

The dark, all he knew was the dark. Nothing responded back, and nothing ever would.

Max had buried him, and as he cradled Julia in front of a warm campfire on a long Spanish summer evening they both looked deep into the flames and sighed.

'Time to sleep my love'
'Time to sleep indeed'

And they both went off to dance with the Angels at rest, as Max's soul kept guard over the monsters cage, forever.

THE END

Made in the USA
Monee, IL
23 November 2022

18356051R00042